THE
CAPITAL
CATCH

Also by David A. Kelly

BALLPARK MYSTERIES

THE MVP SERIES

Babe Ruth and the Baseball Curse

BALLPARK Mysteries 13

THE CAPITAL CATCH

by David A. Kelly

illustrated by Mark Meyers

A STEPPING STONE BOOK™
Random House New York

*This book is dedicated to my best friend and college roommate,
Waleed Abdalati, with whom I have explored many places over the years,
including Washington, D.C.*
—D.A.K.

To Paul & Betty, thank you for all the support!
—M.M.

"You can't hit what you can't see."
*—Walter "The Big Train" Johnson,
Hall of Fame pitcher for the Washington Senators, 1907–1927*

Text copyright © 2017 by David A. Kelly
Cover art and interior illustrations copyright © 2017 by Mark Meyers

All rights reserved. Published in the United States by Random House Children's Books, a division of Penguin Random House LLC, New York.

Random House and the colophon are registered trademarks and A Stepping Stone Book and the colophon are trademarks of Penguin Random House LLC. Ballpark Mysteries® is a registered trademark of Upside Research, Inc.

Visit us on the Web!
SteppingStonesBooks.com
randomhousekids.com

Educators and librarians, for a variety of teaching tools, visit us at RHTeachersLibrarians.com

Library of Congress Cataloging-in-Publication Data is available upon request.
ISBN 978-0-399-55189-5 (trade) — ISBN 978-0-399-55190-1 (lib. bdg.) —
ISBN 978-0-399-55191-8 (ebook)

Printed in the United States of America
10 9 8 7 6 5 4 3 2 1

This book has been officially leveled by using the F&P Text Level Gradient™ Leveling System.

Random House Children's Books supports the First Amendment and celebrates the right to read.

Contents

A Surprise Catch

"Who wants to meet the president of the United States?" the Secret Service agent asked.

Mike Walsh and his cousin Kate Hopkins raised their hands and jumped up and down. They were standing outside the gates to the White House in Washington, D.C., waiting for a tour.

"We do! We do!" Kate called out. Her brown ponytail bounced as she jumped.

The Secret Service agent guarding the entrance smiled and shook her head. "Sorry," she said. "I'm just seeing who's paying attention. Unfortunately, you don't get to meet the president on a White House tour. But you will see where he lives!"

"Drat!" Mike said. He tossed a worn baseball from hand to hand. "That would have been so cool. Maybe the president would have signed my baseball!"

"Maybe you can get an autograph from a player at tonight's game," Mrs. Hopkins said.

Mike and Kate had come to Washington, D.C., from their home in Cooperstown, New York, the day before with Kate's mother, Mrs. Hopkins. Kate's mom was a sports reporter for American Sportz. She had brought them down to see two games between the Washington Nationals and the Arizona Diamondbacks, and to take a tour of the Nationals stadium. The first baseball game was that night, but they were spending the day sightseeing. They were starting with a tour of the White House.

The Secret Service agent whistled loudly. "Okay, everyone line up," she said. The tour group gathered against the black iron fence outside the White House. A different Secret Service agent checked bags and asked people their names.

"Boy, I'm glad we're not bringing D.C.'s baseball team with us on the tour," Mike whispered to Kate as they approached the checkpoint.

"Why?" Kate asked.

"Because the Secret Service agents probably wouldn't let them in!" Mike said. "D.C.'s baseball team has moved and changed its name so many times over the years that the Secret Service would be suspicious. The team started as the Washington Senators, but when they moved to Minnesota, they became the Minnesota Twins. There was a second Washington Senators team, but that one moved to Texas and became the Texas Rangers. After that, Washington, D.C., didn't have a team for over thirty years! Then the Montreal Expos moved to D.C. in 2005 to become the Washington Nationals."

"Whew!" Kate said. "That's a lot of different teams and names. Hopefully you can at least remember *your* name when we get to the checkpoint!"

A few minutes later, Mike, Kate, Mrs. Hopkins, and the rest of the tour group were standing inside the White House. As they moved to the first room, Mike showed Kate the baseball he had snuck in. "Keep an eye out for the president," he whispered. "If I spot him, I'm going to ask him to sign my ball!"

Kate brushed him off. "You haven't got a

chance," she said. "I'll bet President Diaz is off traveling or meeting with Congress."

Mike shook his head. "I think he's here," he said.

"Well, at least we'll see his brother, Chip, at the game tonight," Kate said. Chip Diaz was the president's younger brother. He was the catcher for the Washington Nationals and was one of the fans' favorite players.

Mike tossed the ball into his other hand. "Yeah, that's a good idea," he said. "If I get Chip's autograph, at least I'll have the president's *last* name on my ball!"

The tour group walked down a long hallway. As they walked, Kate pointed to the paintings of past presidents on the walls. "Hey, don't forget there are going to be lots of presidents at the Nationals' baseball game," she said. "Maybe one of them could sign your ball."

Mike's eyes opened wide. "Good idea!" he said. "I forgot about the racing presidents!" During each Nationals home game, mascots dressed as presidents—such as Lincoln, Washington, and Jefferson—raced through the ballpark. The mascots wore old-fashioned clothes and had huge foam heads. They looked really silly, and the fans loved them.

The next stop on the tour was a big room with fancy curtains and lots of antiques. The walls and furniture were all bright red. "This is called the Red Room," the tour guide said. "It's been used as a music room, as a living room, for small dinner parties, and more."

Mike, Kate, and the rest of the tour group explored the room. Mike headed for a doorway that was blocked off with a red velvet rope.

"I'm afraid that's off-limits," the tour guide said when she spotted Mike near the rope.

Mike nodded and stepped away. He walked over to Kate and nudged her. "Hey, what if we stay behind and play catch in here?" he asked. "Then we could say we've played baseball in the White House!"

Kate shook her head. "You're crazy! We'd get thrown out!" she said.

A few minutes later, as the tour group continued on to the next room, Mike lingered behind. When the room was empty, he pretended to play a baseball game by himself. Mike wound up to pitch his ball. Instead of throwing it, though, he held it at eye level and ran from one side of the room to the other. Then he swung a pretend bat to make a hit. But as he twisted his wrists, the baseball slid out of his hands.

Mike gasped. The ball bounced on the rug. It rolled under a red velvet rope that stretched across an open doorway, then disappeared.

Mike froze.

No alarms went off. Mike could hear the tour guide in the next room talking about a piece of furniture. He tiptoed forward to look for his ball.

When he got to the doorway, he dropped down to his hands and knees to crawl under the red velvet rope.

"HALT RIGHT NOW!" called a voice.

A Secret Service agent stepped in front of Mike. "You can't do that," she said. "This room is off-limits!"

Mike crawled backward and then stood. His cheeks blushed bright red and his freckles stood out. "Um, sorry," he said. "I was just trying to get my baseball."

The agent waved Mike along. "You'll have to catch up with your tour group," she said.

Mike tried to peek around the agent to look for his ball, but he couldn't spot it. The agent took a step forward. "You need to leave *now*," she said in a flat tone of voice.

Mike's shoulders slumped. He turned to go, walking slowly toward the tour guide's voice in the next room. But before Mike had gone more than a few steps, there was a soft voice from behind him.

"Excuse me," said the voice. "Is this yours?"

Mike turned around. His jaw dropped.

The president of the United States was holding Mike's baseball!

A Presidential
Secret

President Diaz was standing in front of the security guard who had just shooed Mike away. The president had jet-black hair and big brown eyes. He held Mike's baseball in his hand.

Mike nodded. "Uh, yes, Mr. President, that's mine," he said.

President Diaz tossed the baseball. Mike held up his hands and caught it easily.

"Nice catch!" the president said. "You should play for the Washington Nationals!"

Mike smiled. "I don't think I'm old enough

for that yet, sir," he said. "But my cousin Kate and I are going to the Nationals game tonight! We're going to try to get your brother's autograph. But I'd really like to get yours! Would you sign my baseball?"

"Sure," the president said. "Do you have a pen?" He walked across the room to Mike.

Mike nodded. He fumbled to get his pen out of his back pocket. The security guard took a few steps closer and watched Mike closely.

President Diaz signed a big *President Diaz* on the ball's sweet spot. He handed the ball back to Mike. Then he leaned over and asked, "Do you want to know a secret?"

Mike nodded eagerly.

"You have to promise not to tell," the president said.

Mike held up his left hand. "I promise!" he said. "My cousin Kate and I are detectives, so we're really good at keeping secrets and solving mysteries."

The president's right eyebrow went up a little bit. "Detectives?" he said. He thought for a moment. "That's very interesting, because I

14

know someone who could use a good detective."

"Really?" Mike asked. "Kate and I have solved a *lot* of baseball mysteries."

President Diaz tapped his foot a few times. "I need you to help my brother, Chip. Someone's stealing his equipment, and it is interfering with his game. If he doesn't start playing better, his coach may send him back to the minors," the president said. "I think he's having trouble because someone's stolen his batting gloves, a hat, his travel bag, and a bunch of other stuff. Maybe you and Kate can stop by the Nationals' clubhouse before the game to investigate. I'll tell him you're coming."

President Diaz pulled a piece of paper out of his pocket. He wrote down a number and handed it to Mike. "Here's a phone number where you can reach my secretary," he said.

Mike nodded. "Kate and I will do our best,"

he said. He tucked the paper in his pocket. Then he looked at his baseball. "Hey," he said. "Maybe I'll also be able to get your brother's signature on my ball right next to yours!"

The president laughed. "That's a good idea," he said. "But I still have to tell you my secret." He bent over and whispered something in Mike's ear.

Mike's eyes grew wide. "Really?" he asked.

The president nodded. "That's cool! I'm going to make sure to get a picture of it!"

President Diaz glanced at the security guard standing next to him. "Remember, you promised not to tell anyone!" he said. "It's time for me to get back to work. And you need to get back to the tour."

The president waved goodbye and disappeared around the corner.

Later that afternoon, Mike and Kate stepped up to the door of the Washington Nationals' clubhouse. Mrs. Hopkins had taken them to the stadium early for the game. Kate's mother went up to the pressroom to work. But she had gotten special all-access passes for Mike and Kate to explore Nationals Park. They were using them to go to the clubhouse to see President Diaz's brother.

Mike and Kate showed the security guard their passes. After he opened the door and waved them in, Kate asked where they could find Chip.

"Right over there," the guard said. He pointed to a locker on the other side of the room. "I don't know where he is right now, but he should be back shortly."

The clubhouse was buzzing with activity. It was still a couple of hours before game time. The players were starting to get ready. Workers were bringing in equipment and supplies. An electrician, wearing a yellow safety hat, was standing on a ladder fixing one of the TVs. And a bald man in a dark blue suit and red tie stood in the far corner. He was reading a newspaper.

"Look at this!" Mike said when they reached Chip's locker. Chip's catcher's mask hung on the side of the locker. Mike slipped it off the hook and put it on. It was hard to see Mike's face behind all the black bars. He turned to show Kate.

"¡Estás loco!" Kate said. She was learning Spanish. She liked to use it whenever she could. "You're crazy! Take that off. We're supposed to be helping Chip, not playing with his stuff!"

"Yeah, but we're supposed to catch a thief, remember?" Mike said. "Get it? *Catch* a thief?"

Kate groaned. "Yes, Mike," she said. "But you're going to catch some trouble if you don't get that off now!" She pointed across the room. "There he is!"

Chip Diaz was crossing the clubhouse floor with a man in a red polo shirt with a Nationals logo. Chip was wearing his Washington Nationals uniform. The men seemed to be in the middle of a deep conversation. And they were headed straight for Chip's locker!

Mike scrambled to get the catcher's mask off, but the strap on the back got stuck.

"Hurry up!" Kate whispered. "They're almost here!"

Mike tugged at the mask, but it wouldn't come off.

It was too late.

Chip Diaz and his friend stopped right in front of them!

No Problem Here

"¡Hola!" Chip said. "Are you two the famous Kate and Mike that my brother told me about? Or is this a new catcher trying to take my spot?"

"Sorry, I just wanted to try this on and it got stuck," Mike said.

Chip laughed. He leaned over and took the mask off Mike's head. Mike let out a big sigh of relief. Chip hung the mask back up in his locker.

"No problem. Sometimes it's tough for *me* to get it off," he said. "But now you can meet my old college friend, Andy. Andy, this is Mike and Kate. They're friends of my brother."

Andy said hello and shook hands with Mike and Kate.

Chip clapped Andy on the back. "Andy's one of our great tour guides here at Nationals Park."

"Cool! We're taking a tour tomorrow morning," Mike said.

"There's no one who knows history as well as Andy," Chip said. "He's the one to talk to if you want both baseball and history!"

"Washington, D.C., is the best place in the world to learn about history," Andy said. "When you think of it, it's positively presidential."

Chip laughed. "Andy also works at the Lincoln Memorial, so if you have any tricky Abraham Lincoln questions, he's the guy to ask," he said.

Mike took out his baseball. "Well then, you might like this," he said. He handed the baseball to Andy.

Andy's eyes opened wide. He looked up at Mike and Kate. "Where did you get this? It's got the president's signature on it!" he said. "This is really rare!"

Mike smiled. "I know," he said. "I got it directly from the president."

"Do you want to sell it to me?" Andy asked. He took out a wad of bills and waved them in front of Mike. "I'll pay top dollar for it!"

Mike shook his head. "No thanks," he said. Mike reached out for his baseball and took it back from Andy. Then he handed it to Chip.

"Your brother signed my baseball this morning, when I was on the White House tour," Mike said. "I was hoping you could sign it, too."

Chip nodded. "Sure. No problem," he said.

Mike handed him a pen. Chip signed the ball. Andy watched him eagerly. "Chip," he said. "Can you get me a ball like that, with the president's signature? I'd really like one."

"We'll see, Andy," Chip said. "I don't have much time to ask my brother for signed balls. I have to stay focused on my game right now."

Andy nodded. "Okay. It would make a really great addition to my collection." He checked the time. "Oops, I have to lead a stadium tour in a few minutes. Good luck tonight!" Andy waved and left the clubhouse.

Chip turned to Mike and Kate. He crossed his arms and rocked back on his heels. "Now, my brother told me you were coming," he said. "But he didn't tell me why."

Mike and Kate looked at each other. "President Diaz told Mike that some of your stuff has been stolen," Kate said. "Mike and I are pretty good at figuring out mysteries, so I guess your brother thought we might be able to help."

Chip shook his head and smiled. "Stolen, eh?" he asked. He pointed to the bottom of his locker. There was a big flat wooden shelf with nothing on it.

"Like that?" he asked.

Kate tilted her head. "Like what?" she asked. "There's nothing there."

"Exactly!" Chip said. "There's nothing there because my brother thinks my travel bag has been stolen!"

"So the president was right!" Kate said.

Chip let out a big sigh. He slumped down onto the bench in front of his locker. "Not really," he said. "My brother's always trying to help. But sometimes he overdoes it."

"But he also told us you had a hat and bat-ting gloves stolen!" Mike said. "Were they?"

Chip shook his head. "Well, I *have* had some problems *finding* stuff lately," he said. "But it's not because it was stolen. It's lost. I've lost stuff all my life. I used to lose my

homework at school. I lose socks all the time. I'm just losing a little more than usual right now."

Chip moved some of the shirts in his locker. He seemed to be looking for something. "Like my new batting gloves. They have my number, eight, on them. I just opened them yesterday, but I can't find them anywhere," he said.

Mike and Kate watched as Chip rummaged through the drawer under his locker for a minute. But he came up empty. "Like I said, who would steal my batting gloves?" he said. "I must have left them in the batting cage or something."

"When did you start missing your equipment?" Kate asked.

Chip shrugged. "I don't know. Probably about a month ago, when I made a bad play against the Mets," he said. "I started to get nervous that Coach Jimmy might send me back down to the minors. Lately, it's all I can think about. I guess I haven't been able to keep track of stuff since."

"But you're a great catcher!" Mike said. "You don't have anything to worry about!"

"Except pop-ups!" Chip said. "I always have trouble with them. I'm great at bunts and squeeze plays and rundowns. But lately, every time there's a pop-up, I get nervous. I'm worried that I'm going to lose the ball before I can catch it. I just wish I wasn't losing everything lately. It's bad luck!"

"Are you sure no one's stealing from you?" Kate asked.

Chip waved his hand. "Yeah," he said. "I'm sure it's just getting lost. I'm so focused on trying to keep my job that I can't be bothered to keep track of everything."

Mike glanced at Kate.

Chip leaned closer to them. "Listen, I appreciate your concern," he said. "But there's no problem here. My brother is worrying too much. The only reason he thinks my stuff is being stolen is because he's the president and he has to be extra careful."

"What should we tell your brother?" Mike asked.

Chip stood up. "Tell him he's overreacting. Nothing's being stolen," he said.

The Chase

After Chip left, Mike and Kate stared at his locker for a few moments, unsure of what to do.

Then Kate tugged Mike's shirt. "I guess that's it. I don't think we're going to get any further here," she said. "Let's go find our seats and watch the game."

They left the clubhouse and walked up to the hallway that led to the field. Fans were starting to come into the stadium. As soon as they came across a souvenir stand, Mike stopped.

"Hang on," he said. "I want to get a new baseball for other signatures and a holder for my presidential ball."

After Mike made his purchases, they continued toward their seats. All around them, fans with red Washington Nationals jerseys streamed by. Off in the distance, Mike and Kate could see the skyline of downtown Washington, D.C. Kate thought she even spotted the Capitol building.

Suddenly, Mike nudged Kate. He pointed to their right, down to the infield.

"Don't say anything now," Mike said. He continued to point at the field as though he had just seen something. "Just pretend I'm showing you something. Then follow me. Nod your head like you agree!"

"Um, okay," Kate said. She nodded as Mike

told her to. Then she followed him back and forth through groups of fans carrying trays of food.

Mike stopped at one of railings that overlooked the field. "Just keep looking at the field," he said to her. Kate nodded and watched the Nationals players stretch. A few of them got up and ran sprints on the outfield grass.

Mike pretended to continue to look at the field. But as he did, he turned his head slightly and glanced over his shoulder. Then he snapped his head back toward the field and stared at the players.

"What's going on?" Kate whispered.

"Don't look now," Mike said. "But we are being *followed*!"

Kate's eyes opened wide. "What?" she asked. "Where? Since when?"

"Since we left the Nationals' clubhouse," he said. "That bald man in the blue suit from the clubhouse left right behind us. He's been following us ever since."

Mike pulled the new baseball out of his pocket. He rolled it along the railing a couple times, from one hand into the other. Then he leaned toward Kate. "When I drop the ball," he said, "you follow it and pick it up. Then take a look at the man in the blue suit."

Mike let the ball drop to the ground. It rolled across the concrete sidewalk toward a trash can. Kate scrambled after it. She stopped the ball with her foot and bent down. As she picked it up, Kate studied the man. He was definitely the one from the clubhouse. He was watching Mike. Kate hurried back to the railing.

"That's weird," she said. "But let's make sure

he's really watching us. Now *you* follow *me!*"

Kate handed Mike the ball and headed off down the walkway. Mike hurried to catch up. As they wound their way through the crowd, the man followed them. When they stopped in front of an ice cream stand, Kate pretended to read all the different flavors. The man waited on the other side of the hallway, a few food stands down.

"He's definitely on our trail," she said to Mike. "Maybe he's the one who's been stealing Chip's stuff! He probably saw us talking to Chip and wants to know what we're doing."

Mike nodded. "Yeah, that's it," he said. "If we catch him, I can tell the president we've solved the mystery!"

"Now's our chance," Kate said. "Let's corner him. We can do it on the count of three!"

Mike nodded. "One. Two. THREE!" he said.

Mike and Kate twirled around and ran directly at the man who had been following them!

When he saw Mike and Kate running toward him, the man dropped his newspaper and spun around. A few steps later, he ducked into a small hallway.

Mike and Kate ran as fast as they could to catch up to him. Their sneakers pounded on the concrete walkway. But suddenly, a school group cut right in front of them!

Mike and Kate made their way through the crowd of kids. Finally, they broke free on the other side.

"Over there!" Kate said. She pointed to where the man had disappeared. "There's a door!"

Mike and Kate sprinted toward the door. It was partway open! They raced as fast as they could, but the door was closing fast.

Kate was in the lead. When they were a few feet away, Kate reached out to grab the handle.

Just as she did, there was a loud *CLICK*!

The door snapped shut.

A Big Loss

Kate grabbed the handle and rattled the door, but it was locked tight. A big sign above the handle read EMPLOYEES ONLY.

"Argh!" Mike pounded his fists on the door. "We just missed him! He *must* be the thief. Why else would he have run away?"

"I don't know," Kate said. "Something's fishy." She kicked at the ground. "We almost had him!"

Over on the main walkway, fans rushed by,

trying to find their seats before the game. Then the loudspeakers crackled and an announcer's voice welcomed everyone to Nationals Park.

Kate shrugged. "I guess it's time to find our seats," she said.

Mike nodded. He kicked the bottom of the door one more time, but it didn't open. Then he followed Kate. Their seats were near the third-base line, with a great view of home plate.

As the last strains of "The Star-Spangled Banner" floated through the air, the announcer called, "Play ball!"

The Nationals ran out to their positions as all the hometown fans cheered. Even though it was early evening, it wasn't dark yet. The setting sun had just begun to light the sky pink.

The first Arizona Diamondbacks batter stepped up to the plate. Jason Jackson, the

Nationals pitcher, took the mound. He had a big head of curly blond hair. It poked out from under his red baseball cap. Chip Diaz squatted behind the plate with all his catcher's gear on. He signaled different pitches with his fingers until the pitcher nodded in agreement.

Although Mike and Kate couldn't see the signs that Chip was sending, they were working. The first three Diamondbacks batters struck out!

When they came up to bat, the Nationals were able to get two men on base with only one out. But the Diamondbacks made a double play to end the first inning.

The next inning went by fast, with neither team scoring.

The Diamondbacks almost scored in the third inning, but Chip made an amazing play.

The Diamondbacks had runners on first and second with two outs when their batter hit a high pop-up. As it arced sideways down the first-base line, Chip jumped up and ripped off his catcher's mask. He followed the ball toward the stands. Chip stretched his glove over his head and shifted as the ball came down. Even though it was headed for the first row of seats, Chip kept going. At the last minute, he dove over the infield wall. Chip's glove stretched toward the ball as his body crumpled into a fan's lap!

The crowd gasped!

But a moment later, Chip pushed himself up and held out his glove. The ball was in it!

The inning was over, and the Diamondbacks had not scored! The crowd went wild with cheers as the Nationals jogged off the field.

The play seemed to energize the Nationals,

who scored two runs in the bottom of the third inning, to pull ahead 2–0.

Halfway through the fourth inning, Mike and Kate heard everyone clap and yell. They looked around to see what was going on. The Nationals had just come off the field.

"It's time for the Presidents Race!" Mike said. He pointed to the giant video screen behind center field. It showed four presidents with giant foam heads outside the Capitol building.

"Look, it's Washington, Jefferson, Lincoln, and Teddy Roosevelt," Kate said. "I read that Teddy almost never wins. Come on, Teddy!"

On the screen, the presidents lined up. And they were off! The video showed them running past famous sights in Washington, D.C. Then they burst out of a door in right field and raced toward home plate!

The presidents jockeyed for the lead. Mike and Kate laughed along with the rest of the fans at the presidents' big foam heads.

"Those are great!" Mike said. "Imagine how smart I'd be if my head was *that* big! I'd never have to study because I'd be able to remember everything!"

Although the presidents switched leads a few times, it looked like Teddy might win as they rounded home plate and headed for the red finish line. He was far out ahead of the others!

The crowd screamed, "TED-DY! TED-DY! TED-DY!"

Just before Teddy reached the finish line, a giant mascot monkey jumped out of the stands and knocked Teddy over!

Kate gasped. But then she started laughing as the monkey screeched and jumped around while Teddy struggled to get up.

Mike kept cheering for Teddy, but one by one, the other racing presidents zoomed past him.

Moments later, George Washington won the race! The crowd clapped and hooted as the presidents disappeared. "That was cool," Mike said. "But just wait until tomorrow's race. President Diaz told me a special secret about what's going to happen!"

"What secret?" Kate asked. "Tell me! Tell me!"

Mike shook his head. "I can't!" he said. "The president told me not to tell anyone."

A minute later, the Diamondbacks took the field for the bottom of the fourth inning. For the next few innings, the Nationals kept their lead of two runs. But then they changed pitchers, and the Diamondbacks scored two runs in the eighth inning to tie the game!

It would all come down to the ninth inning.

The Diamondbacks were up first. Two batters struck out, but then the Diamondbacks got two men on base. With runners on second and third and two outs, the Diamondbacks batter hit a pop-up.

Chip flung off his mask and charged out of his crouch. As he ran in front of home plate, the base runners zoomed forward. The man on third ran for home. The man on second ran for third. The ball arced up and then started to drop down near home plate.

It should have been an easy out for Chip. The ball was headed right for his glove. Chip lined it up and got ready.

But as the ball approached, Chip shifted slightly left. The ball hit the edge of his glove.

It bounced off!

The first Diamondbacks runner crossed home

plate. The Diamondbacks were now ahead, 3–2.

The ball landed on the ground and rolled toward first base. As Chip chased after it, the second runner crossed home plate. Now the Diamondbacks were ahead 4–2.

Chip finally picked the ball up and threw it to the pitcher, who was standing at home plate.

The players returned to their positions while Chip stood near home plate and stared at his glove. After a moment, he whipped it off and threw it on the ground! Then Chip walked away while the pitcher and other players tried to look busy. The umpire started to walk over to Chip, but Chip waved him off and went to pick up his glove.

The game started again, and the Nationals were able to get the next batter out to end the top of the inning. But the damage had been done. Chip's error might cost his team the game. The Nationals needed to score two runs to tie, and three to win.

But that's not the way it went. The first two Nationals batters struck out. Chip was up third. As he walked to the plate, Mike jumped out of his seat. He pulled Kate's arm and urged her to stand. The crowd was cheering in the hopes that Chip would get a hit.

But Mike wasn't cheering for Chip like the rest of the fans. Instead, he pointed to an aisle behind home plate. Halfway up the aisle was the man in the blue suit they'd been chasing earlier!

"Look!" Mike cried. "It's him again. He's watching Chip!"

As Chip took practice swings at the plate, the bald man in the suit kept scanning the stadium with his eyes and checking on Chip.

"Come on," Mike said. "Let's go get him!"

Mike and Kate scrambled out of their seats. But as they ran up the steps, Chip swung at the first pitch and popped out!

The game was over. The Nationals lost.

Mike and Kate continued to run toward the man in the suit, but soon they were stuck behind all the fans who had gotten up to leave. When they finally got to where the man had been standing, there was no sign of him.

"Missed him again!" Kate said. "First he followed us. Then he was lurking near Chip. He's got to be the thief!"

Mike scanned the crowds. But Kate was right. The bald man was gone.

Caught!

"I can't believe Chip made such a big error last night," Mike said. "That was exactly what he was worried about!"

"I know," Kate said. "I hope he doesn't get sent back to the minors!"

It was ten o'clock the next morning. Mike, Kate, and Mrs. Hopkins had just arrived at Nationals Park to take a tour.

"Hey, I know you!" the tour guide said when he saw Mike and Kate approaching. It was Andy, Chip's friend.

For the next hour and a half, Andy took the group on a tour of the stadium. They climbed to the upper level, where Andy pointed out how they could see the top of the Washington Monument and the Capitol building.

"The first president to throw out a first pitch was President William Howard Taft in 1910," Andy told the group. "He did it during a Washington Senators' opening-day game. Every president since has thrown out at least one first pitch."

"Wow, I would love to have one of those baseballs," said a woman in the tour group.

"So would I," Andy said. "I collect presidential souvenirs. I don't have any presidential baseballs, but I do have a great collection of campaign pins."

After touring the luxury suites, Andy led

the group down to the field, where they took pictures in the dugout. Mike asked if they could go into the bull pens and throw a few practice pitches, but Andy said no. Visitors weren't allowed there.

The tour concluded at the gift shop near the front entrance.

"Thanks for the tour, Andy," Mike said.

"You're welcome," Andy replied. "And, hey, I'm still interested in buying that baseball signed by President Diaz. Let me know if you want to sell it."

"Not right now," Mike said. "But I'll think about it. We're heading out to look at the monuments."

"Sounds good," Andy said. "If you change your mind, I'll be working at the gift shop in the Lincoln Memorial all afternoon."

Kate stepped closer to Andy. "Hey, before we leave, can we talk to you about something?" she asked. "We're worried about Chip. We've heard that some of his equipment is being stolen. But he's not telling anyone about it. He says it's just lost!"

Mike nodded. "Yeah, we wanted to know if you've seen anyone suspicious around Chip who might be stealing his stuff."

Andy folded his arms in front of him and leaned back against the railing to think. He nodded slightly. "You know," he said, "I've been thinking that something's up with Chip. He told me the same thing he told you, that he's just losing stuff. But *I* think someone's stealing it!"

Kate looked at Mike. "That's what we thought!" she said.

"That's why I've been stopping by the

clubhouse a lot lately," he said. "I've been try-ing to check on Chip's stuff before and after my tours."

Kate pulled Mike in closer to Andy. "We think we found out who's doing it!" she said.

Andy straightened up. "What?" he asked. "Who?"

"It's the bald man we saw in the clubhouse yesterday, wearing a blue suit and red tie," she said. "After we left, he followed us around the stadium."

Andy's face grew serious. "That's Mr. MacKay. He's new around here. I think you should check him out."

Mike and Kate nodded. "We're going to see if we can find him at tonight's game," Mike said.

"Good idea," Andy said. "Let me know if you learn anything."

After Andy left, Mike and Kate waited for Kate's mother to make a phone call. Down on the infield, some of the Washington Nationals players were taking batting practice.

Mike and Kate leaned over the railing and watched the players hit. The bright late-morning sun warmed the stadium.

Kate nudged Mike. She pointed to one of the Nationals players walking up to home plate. "Hey, that's Chip," she said.

Even though he couldn't hear them, Mike and Kate cheered for Chip.

"Woo-hoo! Chip!" Kate called. "Knock one out of the park!"

"Hey, up here!" Mike yelled. He stomped on the ground with his sneaker. "Hit one up here!"

Chip let a few pitches fly by. But on the third one, he swung and nailed a long line drive into left field. Mike and Kate clapped.

As they watched Chip go back to his batting stance, Kate gasped. She pointed to the other side of the stadium.

"It's him!" she said. "It's Mr. MacKay, the man who was following us yesterday!"

Mike tugged her shirt. "Quick, there's no time to lose," he said. "Let's go sneak up on him!"

They took off running. Their sneakers pounded on the ground as they raced around the walkway that circled the inside of the stadium.

When they got close to where Mr. MacKay was standing, Mike reached out and stopped Kate. They caught their breath behind a big pillar. Mr. MacKay was standing with his back to them.

On the count of three, Mike and Kate burst

from behind the pillar. They ran at Mr. MacKay from both sides so he couldn't escape. By the time he turned and realized what was happening, it was too late!

They skidded to a halt right in front of Mr. MacKay.

"We caught you!" Mike said.

"Why were you chasing us?" Kate demanded.

MacKay stared back at Mike and Kate without answering.

"Were you afraid that we'd discovered you're the clubhouse thief?" Mike asked.

"And that we'd report you to the *president of the United States* for stealing Chip's things?" Kate asked.

MacKay's eyebrows went up. "What?" he asked as he studied Mike's and Kate's faces.

Then he burst out laughing!

"You think I'm stealing Chip's things?" he asked. "That's good. Wait until the president hears about that."

"Huh?" Kate asked. "You know the president, too?"

MacKay stopped laughing. A big smile

filled his face. "Of course I do," he said. "But you can't tell anyone."

"Tell anyone what?" Kate asked.

"What I'm doing is a secret. But I'm not stealing Chip's stuff," the man said. He offered his hand for a handshake. "I'm Agent MacKay, Secret Service."

"Wow!" Mike said as he shook his hand. "I'm Mike, and this is my cousin Kate." Kate shook Agent MacKay's hand as well. "I met the president yesterday. He asked us to figure out who was stealing Chip's stuff."

"That's funny," he said. "I'm watching Chip, too! The president asked me to keep an eye on him because he thought someone might be after Chip. I followed you yesterday because I wasn't sure who you were." He laughed. "You two gave me a run for my money. I can see why the president asked you to investigate."

Kate pointed to Chip down at home plate. "So does he know you're keeping an eye on him?" she asked.

"No," Agent MacKay said. "And we need to keep it that way. The Nationals owner knows. But everyone else on the team thinks I'm working on a special project for the owner."

"Well, last night we thought you might be the one stealing Chip's stuff," Kate said. "But I guess not. Any idea who might be?"

"No," Agent MacKay said. "But it has to be someone who has access to the clubhouse."

He rummaged around in his pocket and pulled out a scrap of paper. "I did find something this morning near Chip's locker," he said. "But I'm not even sure it's a clue."

He handed the paper to Kate. On the top, it had pictures of Abraham Lincoln, George Washington, and Thomas Jefferson, with a line across the page underneath them. Scrawled on the paper were the words *LM 3:00 p.m. Friday.*

A Surprising
Discovery

"I don't have time to chase down this clue," Agent MacKay said. "I'm busy protecting Chip. Maybe you two can do it?"

Kate pulled out her phone and took a picture of the note. "We'll keep our eyes open," she said.

"Sounds good," Agent MacKay said. He looked out at the field. "Chip is done batting, so I've got to move along. Here's my card. Give me a call if you figure anything out or need help."

Agent MacKay headed to the stairs. Mike

and Kate studied the photo of the note. There wasn't much to look at. It just seemed like a piece of paper.

"Maybe it's from the White House," Kate said. "It's got famous presidents across the top. Maybe President Diaz sent his brother a message and that's all this is."

Mike shrugged. "Maybe," he said. "Though it looks like someone named LM is having a meeting at three o'clock. But we don't know where, or who LM is."

"Maybe LM is someone who works for the Washington Nationals," Kate said. "I'll bet Andy would know. We could stop by his gift shop this afternoon while we're sightseeing."

"Good idea," Mike said.

Kate checked the time. "Hey, let's go," she said. "My mom is probably waiting for us at the front gate."

A little after two o'clock, Mike, Kate, and Mrs. Hopkins were in downtown Washington, D.C. They had taken a short ride on the Metro, the subway in Washington, D.C. Their first stop was the National Air and Space Museum, where they saw the Wright brothers' airplane. They also saw Charles Lindbergh's *Spirit of St. Louis* airplane and lots of rockets. They even got to touch a real moon rock!

After that, they walked up the big grassy park that runs through the center of Washington, D.C., to the Lincoln Memorial.

"Hey, this is what's on the back of old pennies," Mike said.

"It must have taken a lot of pennies to build this," Kate said. "It's huge!"

Behind them was a long reflecting pond that stretched toward the towering pillar of the far-off Washington Monument. It seemed like everywhere they looked, there was another important monument.

Mike and Kate scrambled up the marble steps of the building, while Mrs. Hopkins followed.

"Whoa!" Mike said at the top of the stairs. "He's huge!"

In front of Mike and Kate was the biggest

statue of Abraham Lincoln they had ever seen. He was seated in a tall chair with his arms resting on the sides.

"According to the guidebook I read, the statue is nineteen feet tall," Kate said. Before she and Mike went on trips, Kate often read about where they were going. "And look at his hands."

Lincoln's hands hung over the front sides of the marble chair. The fingers in his right hand pointed down, and the fingers in his left hand curled into a fist. "Some people think that Lincoln's hands are forming an *A* and an *L* in sign language, for Abraham Lincoln," said Kate. "I'm not sure it's true, but it could be."

"Hey, you two, how about a picture?" Mrs. Hopkins called out. Mike and Kate turned around and smiled. Then they looked inside the memorial. Kate went off to the side to read the Gettysburg Address carved into the

wall. Then she and Mike read the words to Lincoln's speech for his second inauguration on the other wall.

"There's the gift shop where Andy works," Kate said. She pointed at a small door to the left of the front entrance. "Let's go ask him if he knows anyone with the initials LM."

They went through a bronze door into a small gift shop just off the main floor of the

Lincoln Memorial. The shop was filled with Abraham Lincoln T-shirts, books, and other souvenirs. They spotted Andy behind the counter.

"Hey, it's you two again," Andy said. "How do you like the memorial?"

"It's great!" Kate said. "The statue of Lincoln is huge!"

Andy nodded. "It's really neat to work here. I get to learn all types of things from the park rangers who give tours," he said. "Sometimes I even get to trade collectibles with them. Here, let me show you my collection of presidential campaign buttons."

Andy pulled out a tablet from behind the counter. He tapped on the screen a few times and showed Mike and Kate a bunch of pictures of his collection.

"Wow, that's a lot of buttons," Kate said.

Andy nodded. "There are many stores around here that sell political and sports collectibles, like campaign buttons and signed baseballs," he said.

Kate glanced at Mike and then tapped on the counter. "Speaking of baseball," she said, "we were thinking about Chip's missing stuff. Mike and I wondered if someone with the initials LM might have taken it."

Andy thought for a moment. "I don't know anyone with the Nationals who has those initials," he said. "But you might want to question the batboy. He's new, and the things started disappearing after he started. Plus, he'd have access to the clubhouse, so he'd be able to steal Chip's stuff."

Mike bounced up and down. "We can do that tonight," he said. "What's his name?"

Andy took a pad of paper from near the

cash register and wrote down the batboy's name for them. "It's Larry," he said.

Andy handed the paper to Kate. She looked at it quickly before stuffing it into her pocket.

"Larry will probably be down near the dugout before the game," Andy said. "I bet he did it."

"Thanks," Kate said. "We'll check it out. Let's go, Mike."

Kate was in such a hurry that she practically pulled Mike out of the gift shop. She led him over to a quiet area just behind the Abraham Lincoln statue.

"What was *that* about?" Mike asked. "We were getting good information from Andy on Larry. Why leave now?"

Kate scowled at him. "Because of this!" she said. Kate pulled out the note that Andy had written. She flipped it open and showed it to Mike.

"L-a-r-r-y," Mike read. "Okay, so what?"

"It's not about Larry," Kate said. She pointed at the notepaper. "Look at this!"

There, across the top, were pictures of Abraham Lincoln, George Washington, and Thomas Jefferson!

"This matches the piece of paper that Agent MacKay found!" Mike said.

"Exactly!" Kate said. "*Larry* isn't the one stealing Chip's stuff. *Andy* is!"

"Andy? But why would he steal Chip's stuff? They're friends. He doesn't want Chip to go to the minors," Mike said.

"What if he's stealing Chip's baseball stuff and selling it to pay for all the presidential souvenirs he's collecting?" Kate asked.

Mike thought for a moment and then nodded. "Maybe," he said. "Yeah, I bet you're right! Andy has access to the clubhouse. He's there during the day when Chip isn't. And the note matches the paper at Andy's counter. It sure seems like it could be Andy."

Mike studied the note in Kate's hand. "And if it's Andy, then maybe we still need to look for a person with the initials LM," he said. "He's probably the one who's buying the stuff from Andy."

Kate laughed. "LM isn't a who. It's a where!" she said.

Kate stepped back and pointed at the statue and the walls of the building. "*LM* stands for the *Lincoln Memorial!*" she said. "I'll bet Andy is meeting someone at three o'clock today, right here. In about twenty minutes, he'll probably be selling more of Chip's stolen stuff."

An Interesting Store

"What time is it?" Mike asked Kate.

Kate checked her phone. "It's a few minutes before three," she said.

They were hiding behind one of the big columns in the Lincoln Memorial. By peeking around the column, they could spy on the front counter at the gift shop. It was easy to see Andy as he helped customers and rang up sales.

Kate had told her mother that she and Mike wanted to spend some extra time at the

Lincoln Memorial. Kate's mom had agreed. She told Kate that she'd be waiting outside, exploring the other nearby monuments. Kate was supposed to call her when she and Mike were ready to leave.

For the past twenty minutes, they had been watching every person who went into the gift shop. But they hadn't seen anyone suspicious. Then, a little after three o'clock, a woman in a red shirt walked into the shop. Instead of

browsing or picking up something to buy, she walked right to the counter.

Mike nudged Kate. "What's she doing?" he asked.

"She just handed Andy a bunch of money. He gave her a bag, but she didn't bring anything up to the counter to buy!"

The woman nodded to Andy and left the gift shop. She headed around the corner and down the front steps.

"Let's follow her!" Kate said.

Mike and Kate raced down the front steps. They stayed to the side so they wouldn't be spotted. The woman headed away from the monument.

Mike and Kate ran to catch up. The woman walked through the paths of the park until she came to the main street. She crossed at the light and continued past a row of government buildings. Mike and Kate crossed the street a little bit behind the woman. Once they got to the other side, they paused so they wouldn't be too close to her. The woman continued walking, then turned left and disappeared into a store.

"That store is called Capitol Collectibles!" Mike said. "I think we're on the right trail. Now what?"

Kate tapped her foot. "I've got an idea," she

said. She whispered something to Mike. He nodded. They walked up the street to the corner, and then turned back. Mike took a deep breath and pushed the door open.

The shop was filled with display cases of different types of collectibles. There were pieces of paper with famous people's signatures, and autographed pictures. There were also all types of sports jerseys and signed baseball cards and photos.

"Wow! This is a cool store," Mike said as he looked around.

The woman in the red shirt was behind the counter. "Can I help you?" she asked.

"We're looking for souvenirs," Kate said.

"Then you've come to the right spot," the woman said. "We've got everything from politics to sports. Looking for anything special?"

Mike nodded. "Yup, baseball stuff. Chip Diaz is my favorite player. Do you have anything of his?" he asked.

The woman smiled. "We have lots of Chip Diaz stuff," she said. She pulled out a pair of batting gloves and laid them on the counter. "I just got these in today. They are game-used batting gloves. You can see Chip's number, number eight, right here on the inside."

Kate nudged Mike. The woman showed them a bunch of other Chip Diaz equipment. She had a travel bag, more batting gloves, a catcher's mitt, and even a jersey.

"Do you see anything you like?" the woman asked.

Mike nodded. "Yes, but I have to get my mother to pay for it," he said. "Can we take a picture of the stuff to show my mom?"

The woman nodded, and Kate used her phone to snap a picture.

"We'll be back later," Mike said. "Thanks!"

As soon as they were on the sidewalk and the door to the shop had closed behind them, Mike gave Kate a high five and then hopped up and down.

"We did it! That's all Chip's stuff," Mike said. "Andy must be stealing it and selling it so he can buy presidential souvenirs."

"And I just thought of a way to catch him in the act," Kate said. "Let's go back to the Lincoln Memorial."

Mike and Kate practically ran back to the monument. After they sprinted up the big steps, Kate led Mike to the door of the gift shop. "Quick," Kate said. "Give me your base-ball that's signed by the president!"

Mike fished around in the pocket of his sweatshirt and pulled out the ball. Kate took the ball in the case and marched inside the gift shop. A few customers were browsing, but no one was at the cash register.

"Oh, hey, it's you guys again!" Andy said when he spotted them.

"Yes," Kate said. "We're leaving soon, but since you were so interested in Mike's signed ball, I wanted to tell you a secret."

Andy put his hands on the glass countertop and leaned over. "What?" he asked.

Kate showed him the ball again. "Chip told us he could get the vice president to sign the ball, too!" she said. "So we're going to drop it off before the game at Chip's locker. He said he could hide it there until he got the ball signed. Then it will be worth even more!"

Andy's eyes lit up. "I'll say," he said. "Hey, I was just thinking, I'll be at tonight's game, too. Maybe you could find me and show it to me when you get the signature!"

"Sure," Kate said. She handed the ball back to Mike, who slipped it in his backpack. They headed for the door. "We'll *catch* you later tonight!"

A Capital Catch

"But we don't have any plans to have the vice president sign my ball!" Mike said to Kate as they left the gift shop.

"I know," Kate said. "But *Andy* doesn't know that. What's important is that he knows that your baseball will be in Chip's locker during the game."

"But we can't get into the clubhouse during the game," Mike said. "How will we catch him?"

Kate waved her hand. "Don't worry," she said.

"I think Agent MacKay can help us with that. Come on, I see my mom by the reflecting pool."

After a quick trip to the hotel to change clothes, the three headed back to Nationals Park.

"I'll see you two after the game," Mrs. Hopkins said as they entered the stadium. "Try to stay out of trouble."

Kate gave a big sigh. "We *will*, Mom," she said. She gave her mom a hug. "See you later!"

As soon as Kate's mom headed off to the pressroom, Kate called Agent MacKay. She asked him to meet her and Mike near the stadium's gift shop.

"What's this about?" Agent MacKay asked when he showed up fifteen minutes later. "You said something on the phone about catching a crook. What's your plan?"

Kate whispered something in his ear. As she did, his expression changed from concern to surprise to excitement.

"That's an excellent plan," he said. "I'd be happy to help. Just give me the ball, and I'll call you when it's the right time."

Mike handed over his baseball. Agent MacKay tucked it into his pocket, gave them a wave, and walked away.

"Now what do we do?" Mike asked as they headed for their seats.

Kate smiled and shrugged. "Just wait," she said. "Let's watch the game!"

It was a perfect night for baseball. The sun was starting to set when the Nationals came out to throw the first pitch. Chip took his position behind the plate. He caught the warm-up throws but bobbled a practice throw to second base.

"Chip seems uneasy tonight," Kate said. "He keeps looking over his shoulder like he's nervous."

"I know," Mike said. "Hopefully he won't have any problems."

The fans cheered when the Nationals pitcher threw his first pitch. They grew quiet two pitches later when the Arizona Diamondbacks got their first batter on base. But the crowd exploded in cheers when the Nationals made a double play on the next batter for two outs. A slow grounder to the shortstop ended the Diamondbacks' turn at bat.

Although they got a couple players on base, the Nationals didn't score in the first inning. As they took the field for the top of the second inning, Kate's phone buzzed. She pulled it out of her pocket and answered it.

"It's go time!" she told Mike. "Andy just went into the clubhouse!"

Kate sprang out of her seat and ran up the aisle. Mike followed. When they got to the clubhouse, Agent MacKay was already there. He was leaning against the wall. "Good evening, you two," he said. "At least I think it will be a good evening for Chip when we catch Andy. I'll just wait around the corner here."

Mike and Kate stood against the wall opposite the clubhouse door. Then they waited. A few minutes later, the door opened. Andy walked out. He took a few steps forward and then noticed Mike and Kate.

"Oh, hello there," he said. He dropped his hands behind his back. Then he looked around like he was searching for something. "Why aren't you watching the game?"

Kate spoke up. "We were," she said. "In fact, in the last inning, Chip stole a base! But you wouldn't know that because you were down here stealing something from Chip's locker!"

Andy took a step backward. "What?" he asked. "What are you talking about?"

Agent MacKay stepped around the corner. Before Andy could react, Agent MacKay had

grabbed Andy's wrists and pulled something out of his hand.

It was Mike's signed baseball!

Andy tried to run away, but Agent MacKay held on to his wrists.

"You're coming with me," he said. "I have a feeling you might have given your last tour."

Agent MacKay nodded at Mike and Kate. "Meet me back by the Nationals' dugout after the Presidents Race."

A Presidential Surprise

By the time Mike and Kate made it back to their seats, the Nationals were ahead 1–0. It was the top of the third inning, and the Diamondbacks were trying to catch up.

Kate bounced in her seat. "I can't believe that just worked!" she said.

"I can't believe Andy was stealing from Chip. Some friend he is!" Mike said.

As they watched the rest of the third inning and the top of the fourth, Mike and Kate kept reliving Andy's capture. Mike told Kate how he should've hidden in Chip's locker and jumped out and tackled Andy when he grabbed the baseball.

All of a sudden, the fans around Mike and Kate cheered. It was time for the Presidents Race!

The big video screen showed the foam-headed presidents stretching and getting ready to run in front of the city's government buildings.

"This is it!" Mike said. "Give me your phone. I need to take a picture of this. You won't believe what's going to happen!"

"Okay, but I got pictures of this yesterday," she said.

"You didn't get pictures of *this*!" Mike said. "This is going to be the best Presidents Race ever!"

On the video screen, the presidents took off running! They ran through the streets of Washington, D.C.

Just like yesterday, the racing presidents emerged from a door in right field and raced for home. Teddy Roosevelt pulled out ahead, while Washington and Jefferson trailed behind. Mike snapped photo after photo.

Then out shot someone else. But this racer wasn't wearing a big foam head.

"That's President Diaz!" Kate shouted.

"See? I told you something special was going to happen!" Mike said. He snapped more

pictures and then jumped up and cheered for President Diaz.

President Diaz ran past the foam-head presidents and turned the corner toward home plate. He was ahead of the racing presidents, but Teddy was catching up.

Just after Teddy rounded home plate, he tumbled sideways onto the ground. Then all the other racing presidents, except for President Diaz, tripped over Teddy and went sprawling, too!

President Diaz zoomed across the finish line. He burst through the red ribbon and waved his arms over his head.

The crowd went wild! Mike and Kate cheered.

After the race, Kate and Mike hurried off to meet Agent MacKay at the Nationals' dugout. They found him chatting with Chip.

"These two have something to share with you," Agent MacKay said.

"We caught the person who was stealing your stuff!" Kate announced.

"Yeah," Mike said. "We found your travel bag, your batting gloves, and more at a collectibles shop near the Lincoln Memorial!"

Chip took his hat off. "Really?" he said "That's great! I'll play a whole lot easier knowing I'm not losing my mind."

"We can tell you all about it after the game,"

Agent MacKay said. "But at least you can stop worrying and just focus on baseball."

Chip gave them a big smile. Then he reached out to fist-bump Mike and Kate. "Now I can go out there and win the game!"

"Come on," Agent MacKay said. "We've got another stop to make."

Mike and Kate followed him through the stadium to a large suite that overlooked the field. As Mike and Kate looked out onto the field, someone entered the suite.

It was President Diaz!

"Mike!" he said in a big voice. "It's great to see you again. This must be Kate!" He reached out and shook Kate's hand.

"Congratulations on winning the Presidents Race," Mike said. "That was great!"

President Diaz smiled. "Thanks, but I think I had some help from Teddy," he said. "You never can tell what Teddy will do. There's a reason he's one of my favorite presidents!"

"You made it look easy," Kate said.

"If only winning an election was that easy," President Diaz said with a laugh.

Agent MacKay stepped forward. "Ahem, don't you two want to share some information with President Diaz?"

Mike and Kate looked at each other. "With Agent MacKay's help, we caught the person stealing equipment from your brother!" Kate said.

"Good work!" the president said. "That's better than winning any race!"

Mike and Kate told him how they had discovered Andy was the thief and found the stolen goods. Agent MacKay said he would send an investigator to retrieve Chip's stuff tomorrow. He also told the president that after they

caught Andy with the stolen ball, he confessed. Agent MacKay called the police and had him arrested.

The president gave Mike and Kate high fives.

"That was a capital catch!" he said. "Now I can sit back and enjoy watching my brother play baseball! How'd you like to join me?"

Mike thought for a moment and pretended to stroke his chin like Abraham Lincoln. "I think that's a capital idea!" he said.

Dugout Notes

☆ Nationals Park ☆

Lots of home teams. Over the years, Washington, D.C., has had many different professional baseball teams. The Washington Nationals team played from 1901 to 1960. They were also known as the Washington Senators. They moved to Minneapolis in 1961 to become the Twins. Then the new Washington Senators team played from 1961 to 1971, but moved to Texas in 1972 to become the Texas Rangers. Washington, D.C., also hosted the Homestead Grays from 1912 to 1950. The Grays were an African American team from Pennsylvania that played many of their home games in Washington, D.C.

The presidential pitches. On opening day in 1910, President William Howard Taft started a tradition that still continues. He threw a ceremonial baseball to start the game. It happened at the Washington Senators' Griffith Stadium. Every president since has thrown at least one pitch (although not always in Washington, D.C.). Presidents have done it for opening day, the All-Star Game, and the World Series.

Racing presidents. During the fourth inning of every Washington Nationals home game, there's a Presidents Race. The race features mascots of famous presidents. The mascots have giant foam heads. The presidents who race can change. The current ones are George Washington, Abraham Lincoln, Thomas Jefferson, Theodore Roosevelt, and William Howard Taft. Before Teddy won his first race in 2012, he had a 525-game losing streak!

Stadium with a view. The Washington Nationals' stadium opened in 2008. It was the first environmentally friendly (or green) major-league stadium. The playing field is twenty-four feet below street level, so lots of fans don't have to climb any stairs to get to their seats. The right center field fence also has a small jog, or angle, in it to mimic one that was in the Washington Senators' Griffith Stadium.

Monuments and memorials. Washington, D.C., is full of famous monuments and memorials. Most people know about the Lincoln Memorial, the Washington Monument, and the Jefferson Memorial. But there are others, such as the World War II Memorial, the Vietnam Veterans Memorial, the Martin Luther King Jr. Memorial, and many more. There are also some less-famous ones, like the Maine Lobsterman Memorial, which is a replica of a statue of a lobsterman from the 1939 World's Fair.

The District of Columbia. The Washington Nationals is the only major-league team in the United States that isn't in a state! The stadium is in the District of Columbia. The District of Columbia is a special area where Washington, D.C. (D.C. stands for District of Columbia), is located. It was created so the federal government wouldn't be located in a state.

Take me out to the ball game. The first president to attend a major-league game while in office was Benjamin Harrison. President Warren Harding was the first president to own a minor-league baseball team, and George W. Bush was the first president to own a major-league team.

On the air. Before he was president, Ronald Reagan loved baseball so much that he worked as a radio announcer for the Chicago Cubs.

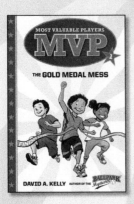

Mike and Kate saw Charles Lindbergh's plane at the Air and Space Museum.

 Read more about him in
THE $25,000 FLIGHT